THE ASTONI AWES

BY MICHAEL CHABON

ILLUSTRATED BY JAKE PARKER

Hi! I'm a superhero. My name is Awesome Man.

I have a cape as
red as a rocket,

a mask as black
as midnight,

and a stylin' letter A
on my chest.

I'm just basically awesome.

I can fly as high
as a satellite

and as straight
as an arrow

or through the time barrier and not get dizzy, or feel sick, or smash
into things . . . except on purpose. When you are a superhero like
me, sometimes you have to smash into things.

I can shoot positronic rays out of my eyeballs. And can I tell you something? Giant killer robots just hate that stuff.

You know what else is totally awesome? My trademark Awesome Power Grip. I can hug a runaway freight train. I can hug jelly.

I can hug mutant talking jelly from Beyond the Stars.

But maybe the most awesome thing about me is my secret identity. Now, this is a total secret, all right? So listen closely, because I'm going to whisper it. Really quietly. So quietly that only you and Moskowitz the Awesome Dog will be able to hear me.

In real life I'm— Uh-oh!

Here comes Professor Von Evil in his Antimatter Slimebot! Antimatter slime is extra gross.

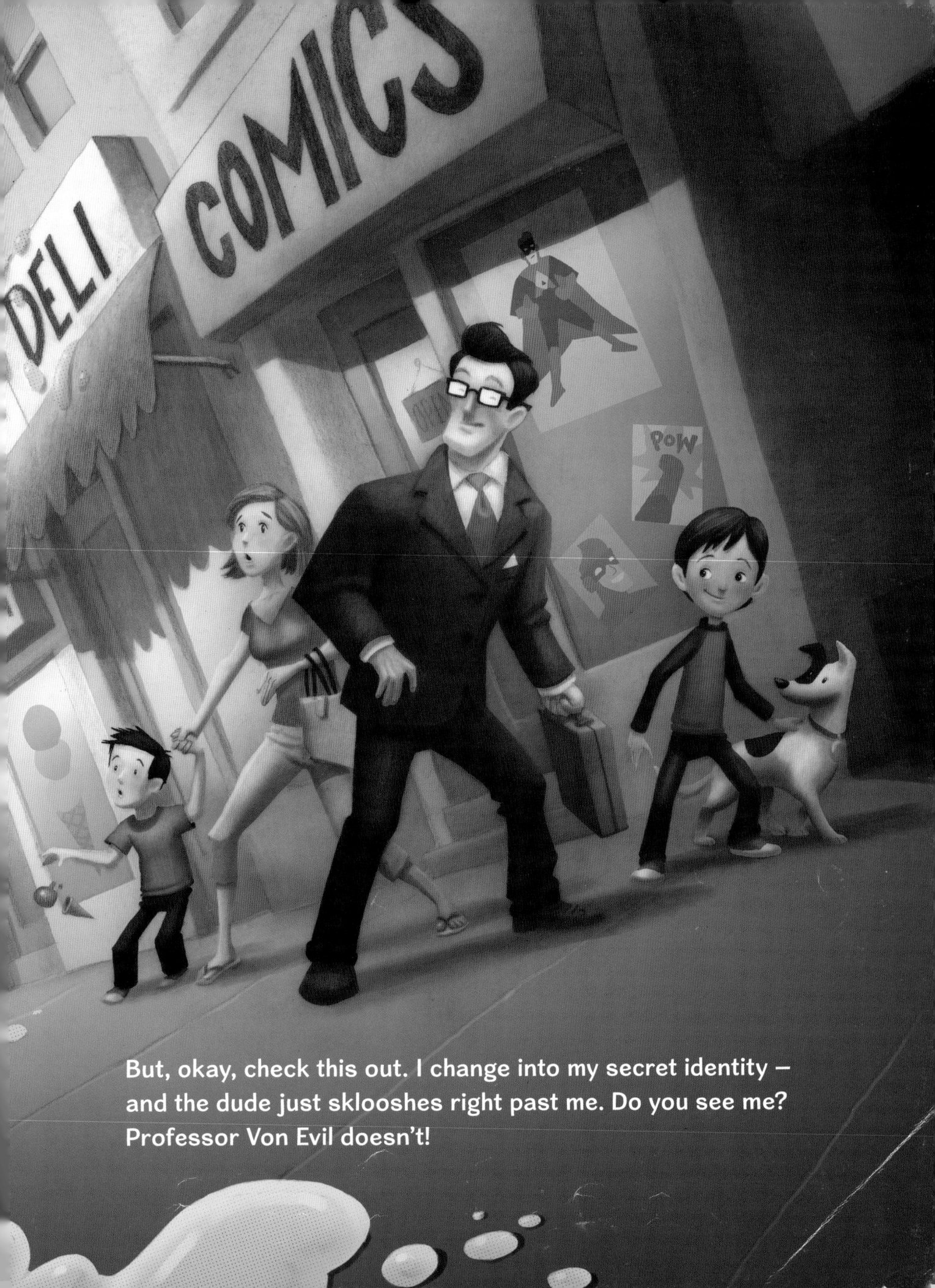

But, okay, check this out. I change into my secret identity — and the dude just sklooshes right past me. Do you see me? Professor Von Evil doesn't!

Then I just sneak up behind him, slap a big old power grip on his pointy head . . . and *SKA-RUNCH!*
"It's time the professor learned his lesson!"

But don't think it's nonstop fun and photons being Awesome Man. Sometimes it can be a pretty hard— What on earth!

Oh man, it's the Flaming Eyeball! My arch nemesis!

I'm going to tell my mu— I mean, I'm going to use
my beams to make a positronic force shield!

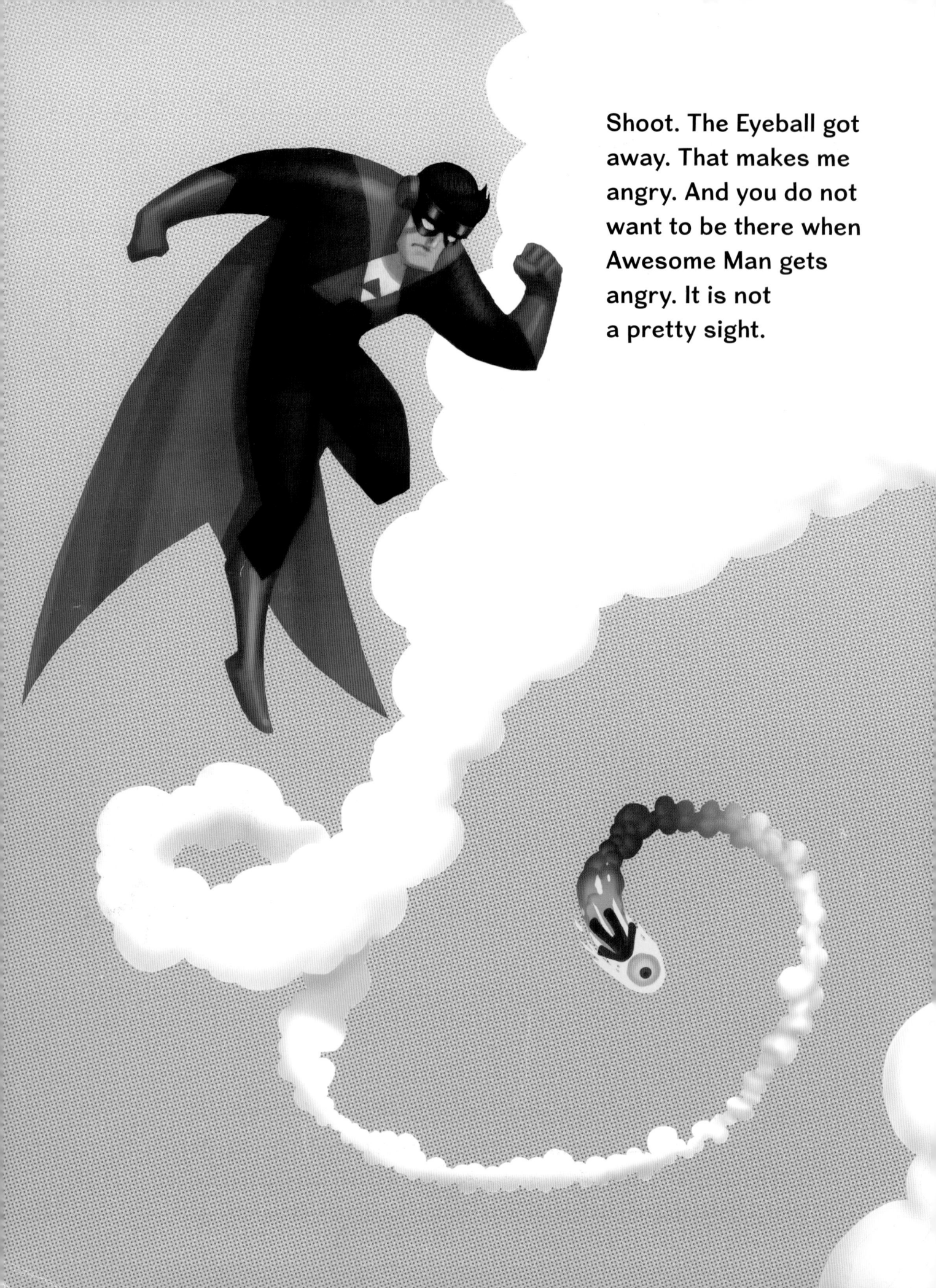

Shoot. The Eyeball got away. That makes me angry. And you do not want to be there when Awesome Man gets angry. It is not a pretty sight.

See, the thing is, I'm super strong. I have to be careful.
I can't start hitting stuff or kicking stuff or throwing stuff
around, even though that's what I want to do so badly.
I might hurt somebody, or destroy a city or something.

So I fly back to the Fortress of Awesome, deep at the bottom of the deepest, darkest trench under the Arctic Ocean. It's peaceful here. Quiet and calm. I can just lie on the bed and chill for a while. I need to get a grip.

So that's what I do. I get myself in a ginormous Awesome Power Grip. It calms me right down so I can think again. And that's when I realise what my problem is: I'm almost out of positrons! All this evil-fighting can make a superhero tired. Really tired. Pooped.

(I love saying "pooped".)

The thing is, it takes a lot of energy to be Awesome Man. To be exact, it takes seven billion kilojoules per nanosecond. But sometimes I get so busy being awesome all the time . . . that I forget.

So I call for Moskowitz on our secret frequency. She brings me a thermovulcanised protein-delivery orb, straight from the kitchen of the fortress. And a little packet of salt.

After I'm all calmed down and positronic again, I take off after the Flaming Eyeball. I fly west. I fly east. I fly eight times around the earth and all the way to the heart of the sun. (The Flaming Eyeball hangs out there sometimes.)

Then I see him! He goes into the hidden entrance of the Secret Headquarters of Worldwide Wickedness. I hide out there and spy on him. He's chilling with Sister Sinister and the Red Shark.

I throw an Awesome Power Grip on all three of them, give them a little blast of eye beams, kick a little bad-guy behind.

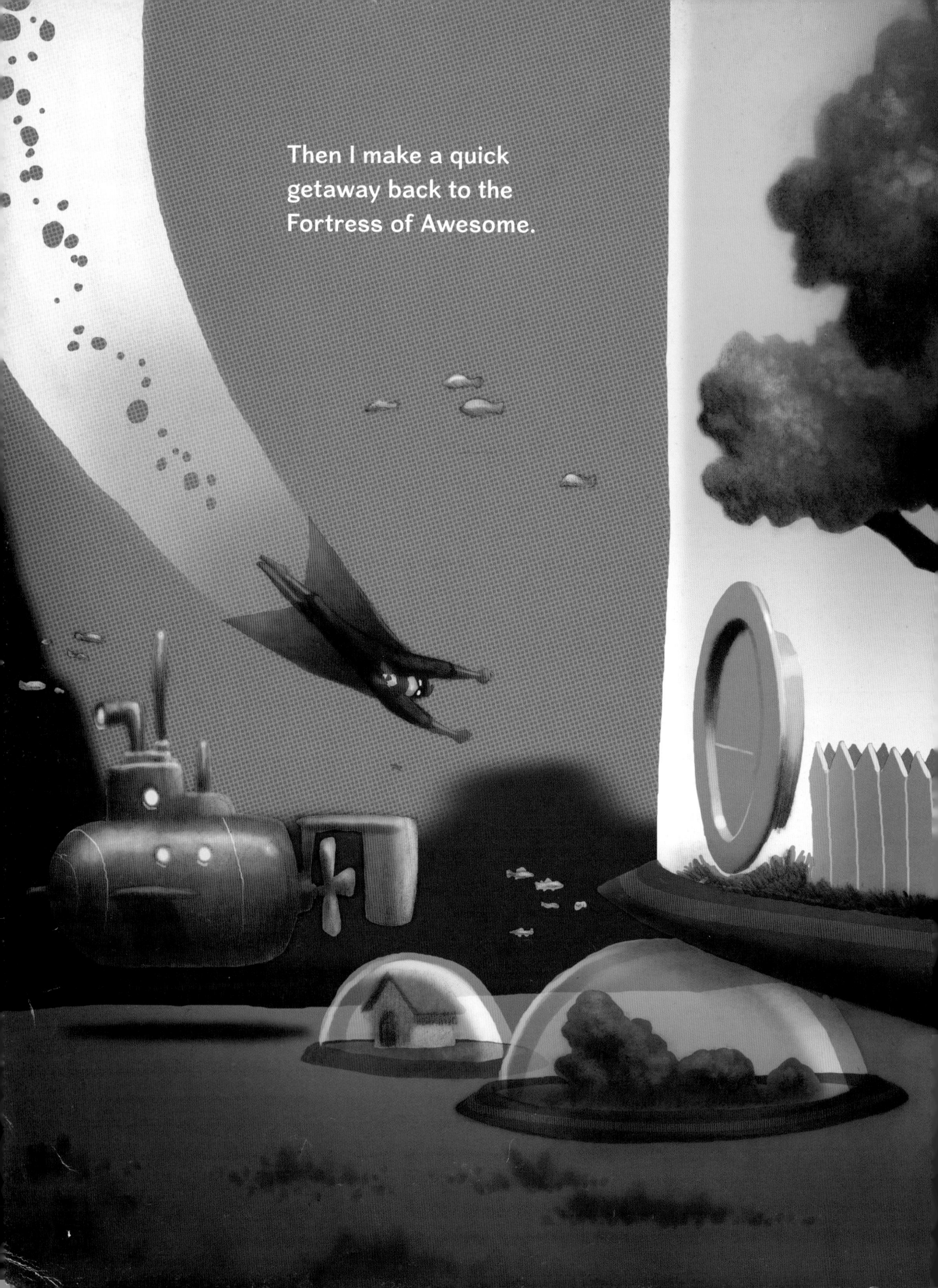

Then I make a quick getaway back to the Fortress of Awesome.

When I get there, my secret identity mum is waiting for me, with a plate of plain old Cheddar cheese and crackers and chocolate milk. I'm so happy to see her, I throw a power grip around her, too.

She says that it feels AWESOME.